You Can Draw

ENCHANTED FORESTS

Laura Pratt

AV2

www.openlightbox.com

AV2

Step 1
Go to www.openlightbox.com

Step 2
Enter this unique code
ARJKO9NA1

Step 3
Explore your interactive eBook!

CONTENTS

- 4 Enchanted Forests
- 6 What Is a Fairy?
- 10 What Is a Dragon?
- 14 What Is a Gnome?
- 18 What Is a Magical Tree?
- 22 What Is a Troll?
- 26 What Is a Unicorn?
- 30 Quiz Yourself on Enchanted Forests

AV2 is optimized for use on any device

Your interactive eBook comes with...

Contents
Browse a live contents page to easily navigate through resources

Audio
Listen to sections of the book read aloud

Videos
Watch informative video clips

Weblinks
Gain additional information for research

Slideshows
View images and captions

Try This!
Complete activities and hands-on experiments

Key Words
Study vocabulary, and complete a matching word activity

Quizzes
Test your knowledge

Share
Share titles within your Learning Management System (LMS) or Library Circulation System

Citation
Create bibliographical references following the Chicago Manual of Style

This title is part of our AV2 digital subscription

1-Year 3–8 Subscription
ISBN 978-1-7911-3306-1

Access hundreds of AV2 titles with our digital subscription.
Sign up for a FREE trial at www.openlightbox.com/trial

ENCHANTED FORESTS

You Can Draw

CONTENTS

2	AV2 Book Code
4	Enchanted Forests
6	What Is a Fairy?
10	What Is a Dragon?
14	What Is a Gnome?
18	What Is a Magical Tree?
22	What Is a Troll?
26	What Is a Unicorn?
30	Quiz Yourself on Enchanted Forests
31	Key Words
31	Index

ENCHANTED FORESTS

An enchanted forest is not a real place. It is a place made up of **characters** and creatures from fairy tales and ancient **folktales**. For centuries, storytellers have set their tales in this magical landscape because of the endless adventures that can unfold there.

An enchanted forest is a place of magic and fantasy. It is where fairies live, along with unicorns, gnomes, trolls, and all manner of monsters. Anything can happen in these charmed locations and does. Horses can fly, wolves can carry princesses on their backs, and birds can share secrets with humans. It is a wonderful land of make-believe.

YOU CAN DRAW

WHY DRAW?

triangle

Drawing an enchanted forest and the creatures living there will spark your **imagination** and creativity. As you draw the pictures in this book, think about what it would be like to live in a land of enchantment. Think about the type of magic you would possess and what you would do with it.

Look around you. The world is made of shapes and lines. By combining simple shapes and lines, anything can be drawn. A house, for instance, might have square windows and a rectangular door. An ogre's ear may look like a triangle. Almost anything, no matter how complicated, can be broken down into simple shapes.

square

rectangle

What shapes do you see in this dragon?

ENCHANTED FORESTS

What Is a FAIRY?

A fairy looks much like a tiny version of a human being and is usually female. While fairies are generally thought to be helpful creatures, they were originally depicted as mischievous and mean. In some ancient **cultures**, people believed fairies kidnapped babies and bit people. However, one thing a fairy could never do was tell a lie.

Fairies were introduced in **legends** and folklore many centuries ago. They play key roles in fairy tales such as *Sleeping Beauty* and *Cinderella*. One of the best-known fairies is Tinkerbell. She is a character in the story of *Peter Pan*.

Eyes and Ears
Some stories say that fairies have green eyes. Sometimes, fairies are portrayed with pointed ears as well.

Fairy Dust
Fairies are believed to have magical powers. Many fairies perform their magic using fairy dust. Fairy dust is kept in a pouch that hangs around their neck or from a belt at their waist.

Clothing
Fairy clothing is often light and fluttery. Some fairies are portrayed wearing long gowns. Others are described as wearing short dresses. Many cultures believe fairies like to wear green because of their love of nature.

YOU CAN DRAW

Hair
Fairies are most often portrayed as having blond hair. However, in some stories, fairies have black, red, or brown hair as well. As fairies are creatures of the forest, they usually decorate their hair with wildflowers.

Wings
Fairies get from one place to another by flying. Some fairies have insect-like wings on their back. Other fairies are said to use magical powers to fly.

ENCHANTED FORESTS

How to Draw a
FAIRY

1 Start with a simple stick figure of the fairy. Use ovals for the head and body, and lines for the arms and legs.

2 Now, draw the body ovals to make the fairy's arms and legs.

3 Next, draw the face, and outline the fairy's clothing.

4 Next, draw outlines for her hair, hands, and feet.

YOU CAN DRAW

5 In this step, draw the outline for the fairy's wings.

6 Next, draw the jewelry, and add details to the clothing and wings.

7 Add finer details to the face, hair, and clothing.

8 Erase the extra lines and the stick figure.

9 Color the image.

ENCHANTED FORESTS

9

What Is a DRAGON?

Fire-breathing dragons are some of the largest creatures found in the enchanted forest. A dragon usually looks like a long, scaly lizard. The term *dragon* comes from the Greek word "drakon," which means serpent or snake.

Dragons have appeared in the legends and **myths** of almost every culture in the world. In some European myths, the dragon is a symbol of evil. Often, a knight in a European tale makes it his mission to slay a dragon in order to rescue a princess. In Chinese culture, the dragon is thought of much differently. Chinese dragons are a symbol of power and luck.

Fire
Many dragons are feared for their ability to breathe fire. Hot flames bursting from the dragon's mouth can be a deadly weapon. One such fire-breathing monster comes from Greek mythology. The Chimera breathed fire like a dragon but had the body of a lion in the front, a goat in the middle, and a snake at the tail.

2150 BC
The year a fire-breathing dragon appeared in a written text for the first time.

35
The approximate number of times dragons are mentioned in the Bible.

Color
Dragons can be any color, but blue, yellow, black, and red are common. The different skin colors of dragons have different meanings. In Chinese culture, black dragons are powerful spirits, with control over water and storms.

10 YOU CAN DRAW

Wings
Not all dragons have wings, but almost all dragons can fly. Many dragons have large wings that look like those of a bat.

Skin
Dragons can have scales or thick, leathery skin. Some dragons are covered with feathers. Certain types of dragons have a row of spikes extending down their back.

Tail
Some dragons have a long, spiky tail. The end of the tail may feature a large spike or a barbed ball of spikes. Often, a dragon's spiky tail looks very similar to the tail of an alligator.

ENCHANTED FORESTS

How to Draw a
DRAGON

1. Start by drawing stick figures for the dragon. Use ovals for the head and body, and lines for the legs and tail.

2. Draw curved lines around the body ovals to form the head, legs, and tail.

YOU CAN DRAW

③ Next, draw the dragon's feet and face.

④ Next, draw its wings.

⑤ In this step, draw the dragon's teeth, horns, and claws.

⑥ Next, add finer details to the head and wings.

⑦ Add more details to the wings and body.

⑧ Erase the extra lines and the stick figure.

⑨ Color the image.

ENCHANTED FORESTS

What Is a GNOME?

Gnomes are creatures that are believed to live underground. Like fairies, they are similar to humans in appearance. Gnomes are much shorter than humans. A typical gnome is said to have a height of about 6 inches (15 centimeters).

The origin of gnomes is unknown. Some think gnomes were first part of **Scandinavian** folklore, but most European countries have stories about gnome-like creatures. These stories tell of the gnome's ability to protect and heal the animals in the forest. They also refer to the long lives of gnomes. Some gnomes are believed to have lived for more than 400 years.

Hat
Female gnomes are usually shown wearing a green cap on their head. This allows them to blend in with the nature around them. Male gnomes are known for their red, pointed caps.

Arms and Legs
Gnomes are known for their strength. Stories tell of them outrunning animals and lifting seven times the weight that a human can.

18th
The century when people began decorating their homes and gardens with gnome figures for protection.

2,500
The number of gnomes in the world's largest collection of ceramic garden gnomes at Merry Harriers Garden Centre in England.

YOU CAN DRAW

Eyes
Most gnomes are portrayed with gray eyes. They are known for their deep, penetrating stare.

Beard
Most male gnomes are shown with long, gray beards. They may or may not have a matching mustache.

Clothing
Male gnomes are said to wear colorful clothing. They are often portrayed wearing a blue shirt and brown pants. A tool belt normally sits around their waist. Female gnomes prefer to wear clothes that allow them to blend in with their environment. They normally are portrayed wearing long skirts and long-sleeved blouses.

ENCHANTED FORESTS

How to Draw a GNOME

① Start by drawing a simple stick figure of the gnome. Use ovals for the head and body, and lines for the legs and arms.

② Now, draw curved lines around the body ovals for the arms and legs.

16 YOU CAN DRAW

3 Draw outlines for the eyes and beard.

4 Next, draw the gnome's hands, feet, and clothing.

5 In this step, draw the gnome's hat, hands, and belt.

6 Next, add details to the face and boots.

7 Add details to the beard, hair, and feet.

8 Erase the extra lines.

9 Color the image.

ENCHANTED FORESTS

What Is a MAGICAL TREE?

Trees play an extremely important role in an enchanted forest. They provide **canopy** and protection from harsh conditions such as rain and snow. Trees are also a source of fear. They can shelter all kinds of scary things within their dark leafy undergrowth.

In some cases, the trees of the forest are themselves enchanted. They can talk and move their branches. Sometimes, trees use their branches to push people a certain way. They have also been known to uproot themselves to chase after anyone who comes too close.

60,000
The number of different kinds of trees you can find in the world's forests.

180 million
The age of Australia's Daintree Rainforest, the oldest forest in the world.

Roots
A magical tree is able to lift its roots out of the ground. When this happens, the roots act as the tree's legs. The tree can then run after people or simply move to a better spot. Sometimes, the roots are used to curl around people to trap them.

YOU CAN DRAW

Branches
The trees in the enchanted forest have twisted branches that work like arms and fingers. They can reach out and grab objects or push them away.

Trunk
Trees are among the oldest living **organisms** on the planet. Their trunks are gnarled and lumpy. If people look closely enough, they may see a human-like face within the tree trunk. Knots within the trunk open to become eyes. A large hole becomes the tree's mouth.

ENCHANTED FORESTS 19

How to Draw a
MAGICAL TREE

1 Start with a simple stick figure of the magical tree. Use curved lines for the trunk and branches.

2 Draw outlines for the trunk and branches.

20 YOU CAN DRAW

③ Next, draw a face on the trunk.

④ Next, draw ovals for the fruit.

⑤ In this step, detail the branches.

⑥ Next, draw the roots, and add details to the face and branches.

⑦ Add more details to the trunk and roots.

⑧ Erase the extra lines.

⑨ Color the image.

ENCHANTED FORESTS 21

What Is a TROLL?

Trolls are another type of creature common in Scandinavian folktales. In most stories, trolls can be found living in caves, mountains, or isolated woodland areas. They do not like humans and are considered dangerous.

Most stories describe trolls as being slow and ugly. They make up for their lack of beauty by being very strong. Trolls are said to hate sunlight. In fact, if sunlight were to fall upon a troll, the troll would immediately turn into stone.

Face
Male trolls are known for their **grotesque** facial features. All males have long, crooked noses. Some have tusks growing on the sides of their face. Others have only one eye, which is situated in the middle of their forehead. Unlike male trolls, female trolls can be quite beautiful in appearance.

Body
Most trolls have stocky bodies. They are often wider at the abdomen and may have a large belly. Many walk in a crouched position because of their humpback.

Fingers and Toes
A troll has very long arms that can extend almost to the ground. Trolls have only four fingers and four toes on each arm and leg.

YOU CAN DRAW

Hair
Trolls are very hairy. Their hair is quite shaggy and difficult to comb. Some trolls have moss growing on their face instead of hair.

Tail
Some trolls are said to have long tails. They often hide their tail in their clothing.

ENCHANTED FORESTS 23

How to Draw a
TROLL

① Start by drawing a stick figure of the troll. Use ovals for the head and body, and lines for the legs and arms.

② Now, draw curved outlines around the body ovals for the legs and arms.

24 YOU CAN DRAW

③ Next, draw the outline for the troll's face.

④ Next, draw the outline for the troll's hair, fingers, and toes.

⑤ In this step, draw the troll's tail and clothing.

⑥ Next, draw its fingernails. Add details to the face, beard, and toes.

⑦ Add more details to the hair, face, body, fingers, and toes.

⑧ Erase the extra lines.

⑨ Color the Image.

ENCHANTED FORESTS 25

What Is a UNICORN?

A unicorn is much like a horse but with one unique feature, its horn. Unicorns live in enchanted forests but are hard to catch. They swiftly run away from any hunter who tries to capture them. Only a **maiden** who is **pure** in heart can hope to tame a unicorn.

Many ancient texts refer to the unicorn. These works, including the Old Testament of the Bible, discuss the unicorn as if it really existed. Today, the unicorn is only a creature of legends. It is thought to be a symbol of purity and grace.

Hoofs
Some unicorns have goat's hoofs. They are cloven, which means they have two parts. A horse's hoofs, on the other hand, have only one part.

10
The length in feet of a narwhal's horn. The narwhal is sometimes called the "unicorn of the seas." (3 meters)

29,000
The age in years of the fossilized remains of a unicorn-like animal discovered in Kazakhstan in 2016.

26 YOU CAN DRAW

Horn
A unicorn's most remarkable feature is its horn. The horn grows out of the unicorn's forehead. It is usually shown as straight with a spiral groove. In ancient times, people believed that the unicorn's horn had **supernatural** powers. They thought that if the horn were crushed into a powder, that powder could work magic. According to some legends, the powder could turn poison into harmless water and cure many diseases.

Body
A unicorn's body looks like that of a beautiful horse. Unicorns are almost always white. Besides their long white manes, some unicorns are also said to have a beard similar to that of a goat.

Tail
Most unicorns are pictured with a long, white horse's tail. Some, however, are drawn with a tail similar to that of a lion.

ENCHANTED FORESTS

How to Draw a
UNICORN

1. Start by drawing a simple stick figure for the unicorn. Use ovals for the head and body, and lines for the legs.

2. Draw curved lines around the body ovals for the legs and head.

28 YOU CAN DRAW

③ Next, draw the unicorn's mane and ear.

④ Next, draw the outline for the tail.

⑤ Draw the outline for the horn.

⑥ Next, draw outlines for the hoofs.

⑦ Add details to the mane and tail.

⑧ Erase the extra lines and the stick figure.

⑨ Color the image.

ENCHANTED FORESTS 29

Quiz Yourself on
ENCHANTED FORESTS

01 Name two fairy tales that feature fairies.

02 What animal does a dragon look like?

03 Where are gnomes believed to live?

04 Which parts of a tree in the enchanted forest may form its face?

05 What happens to a troll if sunlight falls upon it?

06 What traits or qualities does the unicorn represent?

07 What culture sees dragons as a symbol of power and luck?

08 How do fairies perform their magical powers?

09 What are two differences between unicorns and horses?

10 How many of the enchanted forest creatures in this book have tails?

ANSWER
01 *Sleeping Beauty* and *Cinderella* **02** A lizard **03** Underground **04** Knots are eyes and a hole can be a mouth **05** It turns into stone **06** Purity and grace **07** Chinese **08** By using fairy dust **09** Hooves and horn **10** Three

30 YOU CAN DRAW

KEY WORDS

canopy: the uppermost part of a forest, which provides cover and blocks light from smaller trees and plants
characters: people and creatures portrayed in a work of fiction
cultures: particular groups of people at specific points in time
folktales: a collection of traditional beliefs and stories held by a specific culture
grotesque: strangely distorted
imagination: the ability to form new creative ideas or images
legends: unverified stories handed down from earlier times, usually believed to be based on history
maiden: a young, unmarried woman
myths: ancient stories dealing with supernatural beings and heroes
organisms: all living things
pure: free from sin or guilt; innocent
Scandinavian: relating to people from Norway, Finland, Sweden, Iceland, and Denmark
supernatural: a power that seems to go beyond natural forces

INDEX

culture 6, 10, 30

dragon 3, 10, 11, 12, 13, 30

face 8, 13, 17, 19, 21, 22, 25
fairy 3, 4, 6, 7, 8, 9, 30
folklore 6, 14
folktale 4, 22

gnome 3, 4, 14, 15, 16, 17, 30

hair 7, 8, 17, 23, 25

horn 26, 27, 29, 30

legend 6, 10, 26

Scandinavian 14, 22

tail 11, 12, 23, 25, 27, 29, 30
tree 3, 18, 19, 20, 21
troll 3, 4, 22, 23, 24, 25, 30

unicorn 3, 4, 6, 7, 8, 9, 30

wing 7, 9, 11, 13

ENCHANTED FORESTS 31

Get the best of both worlds.

AV2 bridges the gap between print and digital.

The expandable resources toolbar enables quick access to content including **videos**, **audio**, **activities**, **weblinks**, **slideshows**, **quizzes**, and **key words**.

Animated videos make static images come alive.

Resource icons on each page help readers to further **explore key concepts**.

Published by Lightbox Learning Inc.
276 5th Avenue
Suite 704 #917
New York, NY 10001
Website: www.openlightbox.com

Copyright ©2023 Lightbox Learning Inc.
All rights reserved. No part of this publication may be reproduced, stored in a retrieval system, or transmitted in any form or by any means, electronic, mechanical, photocopying, recording, or otherwise, without the prior written permission of the publisher.

Library of Congress Cataloging-in-Publication Data available upon request.

ISBN 978-1-7911-4833-1 (hardcover)
ISBN 978-1-7911-4834-8 (softcover)
ISBN 978-1-7911-4835-5 (multi-user eBook)

Printed in Guangzhou, China
1 2 3 4 5 6 7 8 9 0   26 25 24 23 22

042022
101321

Project Coordinator: Heather Kissock
Designer: Terry Paulhus

Every reasonable effort has been made to trace ownership and to obtain permission to reprint copyright material. The publishers would be pleased to have any errors or omissions brought to their attention so that they may be corrected in subsequent printings.

Lightbox Learning acknowledges Getty Images, Adobe Stock, and Shutterstock as its primary image suppliers for this title.

View new titles and product videos at www.openlightbox.com